MARVEL HEROES

MOVIE THEATRE STORYBOOK

Adapted by Michael Teitelbaum

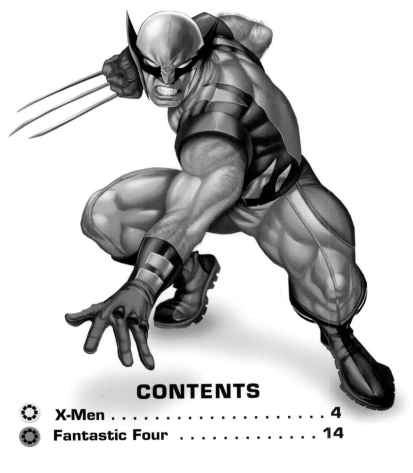

CONTENTS

Reader's Digest
Children's Books®

White Plains, New York • Montréal, Québec • Bath, United Kingdom

D0494835

The X-Men are mutants. A mutant is someone who is born with special powers. For most mutants, their powers begin to come out when they are young teenagers. Because of this, they have trouble controlling their powers. Some are scared by their amazing abilities. Many of these young mutants turned to one man for help.

Professor Charles Xavier, known as Professor X, was also a mutant. He had great mental powers. He could read minds, and send messages into other people's minds.

"Many humans treat mutants badly," Professor X told his young students. "They fear us because they think we are a threat to them.

But I believe that humans and mutants should live together in peace."

Professor X started Xavier's School for Gifted Youngsters. There, young mutants could learn to use DISK 1 their powers. They practiced in 1 ▶ a special training area called the Danger Room.

Professor X assembled a team of mutants, known as the X-Men. Cyclops was the first to join.

"I can shoot powerful beams from my eyes," Cyclops explained, as he shot down a flying target in 2 ▶ the Danger Room. "I have to wear special glasses or a special visor to stop the uncontrollable destructive beams."

Another of the X-Men, Angel, 3 ▶ grew a pair of wings from his back when he was just a teenager.

"I had to practice in secret, learning how to fly," Angel admitted, as he soared high above the others.

The most intelligent X-Man, known as Beast, had mutant powers that allowed him to run fast and gave him great strength and agility. He also looked like a furry blue monster!

"I can also swing from a tree like an acrobat," Beast said, as he swung across the Danger Room.

Jean Grey, another mutant, could also read minds, and move objects with her mind.

"I would like you to join the X-Men, too," Professor X told her.

"I would be happy to join your team," said Jean, as she practiced lifting a two-ton weight using her mental powers. She took the code name Phoenix!

"I can freeze anything, including my own body," the mutant called Iceman told Professor X. "I can use moisture from the air to make an ice slide!" Then Iceman created an ice slide and sped across the Danger Room.

"Not all mutants believe that humans and mutants should live together in peace," Professor X explained to the X-Men. "A powerful mutant named Magneto believes that mutants should destroy humans and take over the Earth. He could become our greatest enemy."

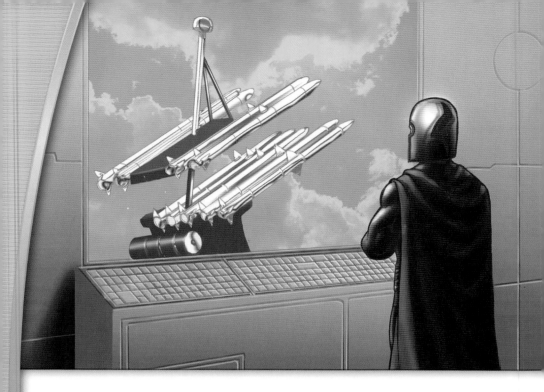

 Deep inside his secret laboratory near the Cape Citadel missile base, Magneto stared at his view screen. On the screen was an image showing a battery of missiles ready for launching at a nearby military base.

"The human race no longer deserves to rule the planet Earth," he muttered, his fists clenched. "The day of the mutants is upon us!" At the moment the missiles blasted off, Magneto concentrated all his mutant power. He sent waves of magnetic energy surging toward the missiles. Magneto's powerful magnetic energy slammed into the missiles, sending them into the ocean, one by one.

"How could this happen?" asked the military base's general. "Nothing could get through our security measures!"

Then Magneto issued his demand. By magnetizing dust particles in the air, he created a grim message in the sky: SURRENDER THE BASE OR I'LL TAKE IT BY FORCE!—Magneto.

"Who or what is Magneto?" the general asked his men.

DISK 2
9

Creating a huge magnetic force field around himself, the Master of Magnetism took over the military base. He sealed himself inside the force field, which now covered the entire facility.

Professor X called the X-Men together. "Magneto has taken over Cape Citadel. You must go there and defeat him!"

The X-Men sprang into action. Arriving at the missile base, they approached Magneto's force field. Angel spread his wings and flew. Beast leaped over a group of soldiers. Just then, an explosion sent a wall of flame toward the soldiers, but Phoenix used her mental powers to save them.

Cyclops fired his optic blast. The powerful beam pushed through the force field and knocked Magneto to the ground.

"Another mutant is attacking me!" Magneto cried in shock. The X-Men burst through the open shield. Magneto fired the base's heat-seeking missiles—right at the X-Men!

The missiles zoomed toward Angel. "Got to dodge them," he cried, flying out of the way. But the missiles gained on the winged X-Man.

"My ice grenades are Angel's only hope!" said Iceman, as he flung the frozen grenades. The ice grenades stopped the missiles—all but one!

Beast swung out from a ledge and caught the final missile with his feet. Then Phoenix used her mind to hurl it into the sea.

"You must be destroyed!" Magneto shouted at the X-Men. Then he sent a flaming tank of rocket fuel hurtling toward the heroes.

"Get behind my shield!" Iceman cried, forming a protective ice barrier.

KA-BLAM! The fuel tank exploded. When the smoke cleared, the X-Men were nowhere to be seen.

"Now nothing will stand in my way!" Magneto shouted.

Suddenly, the X-Men burst from the ground. "Cyclops used his optic blast to dig a tunnel which protected us from the explosion!"

Angel explained. "And now, Magneto..."

But Magneto was gone, propelling himself away from the base using his power of magnetism. The X-Men had won their first battle, but they knew they would face Magneto another day.

Over the years, the X-Men fought many battles. And new mutants joined the team. Among them was Wolverine,

15 who had amazing healing powers, a metal skeleton, and razor-sharp claws. Storm, who had the power to control the weather, could create rain, snow, hail, wind, fog, or

16 lightning. Rogue, who was able to absorb the powers of other mutants, joined soon after.

Despite the years of conflict between the mutants and humans, Professor X still held on to his one main hope: that one day all humans and mutants will be able to live together in peace.

Reed Richards had a dream. The brilliant scientist had worked for years to create a starship that could travel through hyperspace and visit other solar systems. However, Richards experienced one failure after another. Then the government threatened to cut off Reed's funding.

"If I can't prove that my starship works, I'll lose my funding," he said to his best friend, Ben Grimm. Ben had been Reed's college roommate and was a top-notch pilot. "I've got to try a test flight."

"I don't think you should launch that thing, Reed," Ben insisted. "It's a bad idea. The ship's shields aren't strong enough to protect you from the cosmic rays of space! I don't want to pilot that ship."

"The shields will work, Ben," Reed replied. "But if you're afraid to come with me—"

"Afraid!" shouted Ben. "Who are you calling afraid? If you take that ship into space, I'm flying it!"

Reed Richards' fiancée, Sue Storm, also volunteered to go on the test flight.

2 "We've got to take the chance, Ben," Sue explained. "Reed's been working on this for so long. He can't risk losing the funding now. I'm coming along, too."

3 Just then Johnny Storm, Sue's brother, ran into the room. "Hey, don't forget about me!" he said. "Count me in."

"I just hope that those cosmic rays don't kill us all out in space!" Ben grumbled.

4 The four astronauts strapped themselves into the ship and blasted off, zooming into space.

"Everything's working perfectly," Reed said, as Ben piloted the craft toward the stars.

Suddenly, an alarm sounded.

RAAK!-RAAK!-RAAK!-RAAK!

"The cosmic rays are penetrating the ship!" Ben shouted.

"My head is pounding, as if it's going to burst!" Sue cried.

"Ben, you were right!" Reed said. "The shields aren't strong enough to keep out the cosmic rays!"

The four astronauts blacked out. Luckily, the ship's automatic pilot helped the spacecraft make a safe and successful crash landing.

"At least we're all alive," Reed said, as the four astronauts stumbled from the ship.

"But Reed, we've failed," Sue cried. "After all your hard work!"

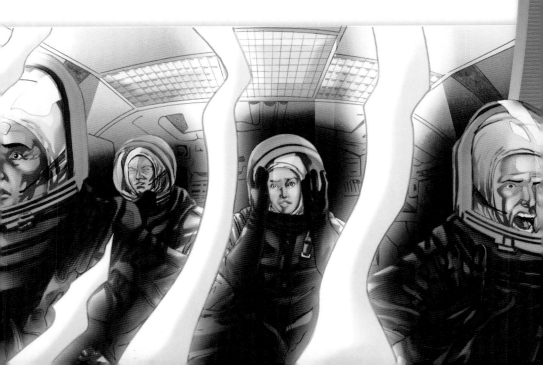

"We still don't know if the cosmic rays affected us in any way," said Reed.

"I feel strange," Sue said suddenly.

7 Then, amazingly, as the others looked on, Sue Storm faded from sight!

"The cosmic rays must have altered your atomic structure," Reed said. "You've become totally invisible."

"Sis!" Johnny cried. "I can't see you at all!"

Then Sue suddenly reappeared.

"What about the rest of us?" Ben asked. "What's going to happen to us?"

8 Suddenly, Ben began changing. He grew in size and his skin turned rocky and orange-colored. "I've turned into some kind of a-a-a thing!" Ben exclaimed. "And it's all your fault, Reed!"

Enraged, Ben grabbed a tree, tore it from its roots, and swung it toward Reed. But Reed's body stretched like a rubber band to get out of the way.

DISK 2

Then Reed's arms stretched like long ropes and wrapped around Ben's body.

"Ben, look! I've changed, too!" Reed cried. "I can stretch my whole body!"

"I'm feeling really warm," Johnny said.

Suddenly, Johnny's entire body burst into flames. Fire shot from his fingertips. He jumped into the air and flew above the others.

"Look, guys!" he cried. "I can control fire. And I can fly!"

When Johnny returned to Earth and his body returned to normal, Reed called the foursome together.

"We've got to use our new powers to help humankind," Reed said. "I'll call myself Mister Fantastic."

"I'm Invisible Woman," Sue added.

"I'm calling myself the Human Torch," Johnny said.

"Just call me the Thing," Ben said.

 "Together, we'll be the Fantastic Four!" Reed said.

Meanwhile, Victor Von Doom, a college rival of Reed's, was performing experiments of his own. One day, one of his experiments caused a terrible explosion. The blast scarred his face. Embittered by the accident, Von Doom turned evil, studying black magic and sorcery. Then he donned a metal mask and began calling himself Doctor Doom.

As Victor Von Doom, he had always been jealous of Reed's success. As Doctor Doom, the evil genius became the sworn enemy of the Fantastic Four.

"I will combine the powers of science with the forces of darkness," Doctor Doom boasted. "And I will use that power to destroy the Fantastic Four!"

And so, the Fantastic Four's greatest and most dangerous enemy was born.